"Michael Jackson showed me that you can actually see the beat. He made the music come to life"

– Rapper-actor P Diddy

04

KING OF POP
MICHAEL
JACKSON
THIS IS IT

MICHAELJACKSONLIVE.COM

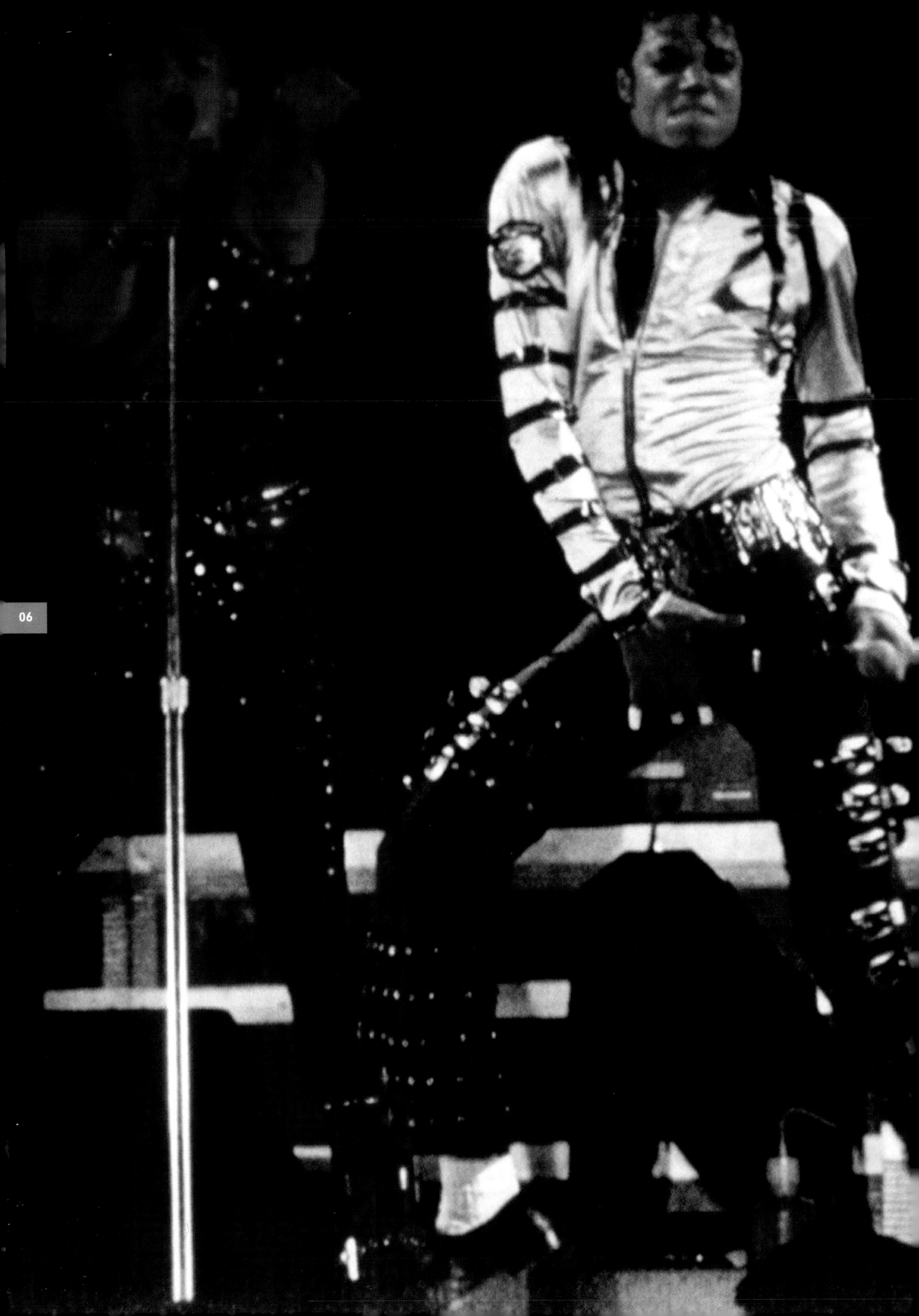

"Just as there will never be another Fred Astaire or Chuck Berry or Elvis Presley, there will never be anyone comparable to Michael Jackson"

– Steven Spielberg

08

He was rightly known as the King Of Pop and the first black American superstar of the MTV generation.
And even though Michael Jackson tragically died aged 50 on June 25, 2009, his legacy of astonishing music will live on.
With global sales of close to three quarters of a billion, and honoured with 13 Grammy awards, he is one of the world's most successful performers and his loss will have as much impact on pop music as that of The Beatles' John Lennon and Elvis Presley. In a career spanning almost four and a half decades, his definitive 1982 Thriller is still the biggest selling album of all time with sales in excess of 60 million. And his collection of 13 US and 9 UK No 1 hit singles includes such classics as Billie Jean, We Are The World and Black Or White. Not only was he an amazing singing talent who made his debut with the family group The Jackson Five when just eight, he was a superb writer of iconic pop songs, including Beat It and Wanna Be Startin' Somethin'. His stage shows were some of the most spectacular ever, an aural and visual delight with Michael taking centre stage in a succession of sensational dance routines. He will be forever remembered for his remarkable moonwalk. And his moves were so sensational that legendary hoofer Fred Astaire once personally rang him to express his admiration. Such was the importance of his visual impact that he also rewrote the rule book on pop videos and recruited such mainstream and acclaimed movie directors as Jon Landis and Martin Scorsese to film such classics as Thriller and Bad respectively. To this day, there are few who will forget the zombie routine of Thriller and Jacko turning into a werewolf at the end. Ironically, he was on the verge of making a major comeback to stadium shows with 50 dates at London's 02 arena, staring next month. Michael Jackson will be greatly missed.

TONY STEWART

CONTENTS

A Mirror publication
Marketing Manager: Fergus McKenna
Mirrorpix: David Scripps and Alex Waters
020 7293 3858

Produced by Trinity Mirror Sport Media,
PO BOX 48, Liverpool L69 3EB
0151 227 2000

Executive Editor: Ken Rogers
Senior Editor: Steve Hanrahan
Art Editor: Rick Cooke
Production Editor: Paul Dove
Editorial: Steve White, Fiona Cummins, William Hughes
Designers: Colin Sumpter, Lee Ashun, Alison Gilliland, Barry Parker
Sub Editors: William Hughes, James Cleary, Mike Haydock

Part of the Mirror Collection
© Published by Trinity Mirror
Images: Mirrorpix, PA Photos
Printed by PCP

STORY OF THE THRILLER

By Daily Mirror journalist Steve White

WORLD leaders – including Gordon Brown – spoke of their sadness over the death of pop superstar Michael Jackson on June 25.

Tributes to "a genius" came from other artists around the world mourning the death of Jackson aged just 50.

Paramedics were called to the singer's Beverly Hills home at about midday after he stopped breathing. He was pronounced dead two hours later at the UCLA medical centre. Jackson, who had a history of health problems, had been due to stage a series of comeback concerts in the UK, beginning on 13 July. Brother Jermaine said: "The family request that the media please respect our privacy during this tough time."

Uri Geller, a close friend of the star, said it was "very, very sad". Speaking outside New York's historic Apollo theatre, civil rights activist Rev Al Sharpton paid tribute to his friend.

"I knew him 35 years," he said. "When he had problems he would call me. I feel like he was not treated fairly. I hope history will be more kind to him than some of the contemporary media."

Melanie Bromley, west coast bureau chief of Us Weekly magazine, said the scene in Los Angeles was one of "pandemonium". "At the moment there is a period of disbelief," she added.

Jackson's life will be remembered on a par with Elvis Presley and the Beatles.

The 50-year-old singer has been referred to as the first black star of the MTV generation, with albums such as 'Off The Wall', 'Thriller' and 'Bad'.

Jackson remains one of the best-selling artists of all time, shifted more than 750 million records worldwide and has 13 Grammy awards.

Born in Gary, Indiana he started out as a fresh-faced boy with the Jackson 5, a group which became a template for future boy bands.

Initially playing bongos and tambourine, the seventh of nine children, he quickly took centre stage. He was only 11 years old when he had his first hit, the Motown classic 'I Want You Back'.

Jackson dazzled alongside his siblings as he passionately begged an ex for "one more chance". The track has featured on Rolling Stone magazine's list of the greatest songs of all time.

The song ABC went to number eight in the UK, selling more than four million copies worldwide. But it later emerged that behind the scenes the story was not so happy and there has been much speculation over the Jacksons' regimented upbringing and the influence of their father.

In an interview with Oprah Winfrey in 1993, Jackson said that during his childhood he often cried from loneliness.

The 1980s were Jackson's heyday, and he Moonwalked around the world to screaming fans, he will be remembered for the groundbreaking videos ones he made for 'Billie Jean', 'Thriller' and 'Bad'.

But as his profile grew, so did speculation over his dramatically changing features, tales of Jackson sleeping in an oxygen tent and rumours that he wanted to buy the remains of the Elephant Man, Joseph Merrick.

MTV today said yesterday in a statement that Jackson "crossed cultural and geographical boundaries, elevated music videos to an art form and was inextricably tied to MTV.

"His music will live on and continue to entertain us forever."

In 1991, 'Black or White' was another big hit, but the lyrics "it don't matter if you're black or white" gave critics another chance to poke fun at his dramatically lightened skin tone.

Jackson denied bleaching his skin and said he suffered from vitiligo.

In 1994 he married Lisa Marie Presley, daughter of rock legend Elvis Presley, but the marriage only lasted 19 months and the pair divorced.

He married for the second time to nurse Debbie Rowe in 1996 with whom he fathered a son, Michael Joseph Jackson, Jr (also known as 'Prince'), and a daughter, Paris Michael Katherine Jackson.

The couple divorced three years later.

Jackson's third child, Prince Michael Jackson II (also known as 'Blanket') was born in 2002. The mother's identity was never released by Jackson,

His documentary with Martin Bashir, 'Living With Michael Jackson', was a PR disaster when Jackson said sharing a bed with a young boy was "a beautiful thing".

The singer kept a low profile following his 2005 acquittal on child molestation charges, after which he spent time living outside the United States.

His last tour was 12 years ago when he played 82 shows in 58 cities for the HIStory tour.

Jackson's planned 50 London shows – titled 'This Is It' – were to mark his first live performance for more than two years.

ON TOP OF THE
WORLD

MEMORIES OF
MICHAEL

BY DAILY MIRROR JOURNALIST FIONA CUMMINS

I CAN still remember each little detail about the first time I met Michael Jackson.

The lavender smell of his skin, his soft voice, the way he spontaneously hugged me - pulling me close to him to him - even though he had never met me before... As I sit at my desk at home and write these words, I can barely believe it. The King of Pop is dead.

Jacko suffered a massive heart attack at his home in Los Angeles but was dead by the time he got to hospital. He was only 50.

In one terrible twist of fate, his life was snuffed out before he had the chance to make his longed-for comeback and prove to the world that he still had it.

He was a conundrum, Michael Jackson. Never quite able to shake off allegations of child abuse, although he vehemently protested his innocence, but one of the greatest entertainers of all time.

We first met at Harrods three years ago when he was in London visiting his old friend Mohammed Al Fayed, the West London store's owner. Jacko agreed to grant me a private audience.

I have met a lot of celebrities over the years but none has quite been able to boast the legendary status of Michael Jackson, arguably the most famous man in the world.

Unusually for me, I was nervous and not quite sure what to expect.

I had read the stories about his plastic surgery gone wrong, the strange obsession with face masks, the Peter Pan syndrome of a boy locked in a man's body...

So it was something of a surprise for me to be greeted by the star with a firm handshake, a smile and a pleasing lack of pretence.

In fact he wore barely a trace of make-up and exuded warmth.

He flung his muscular arms around me in a welcoming hug.

We chatted for several minutes that day and he was alert and interested - and interesting.

I was convinced, even then, that when he finally returned to the stage, it would be to give the performance of a lifetime.

Michael was never afraid of hard work and when he committed to something he gave it his all.

He never did things by halves, that was it. He wanted to prove that he could still dance and sing with the best of them.

But now he will never make that triumphant return to the glory days that we were all hoping for.

The world has lost one of its brightest stars.

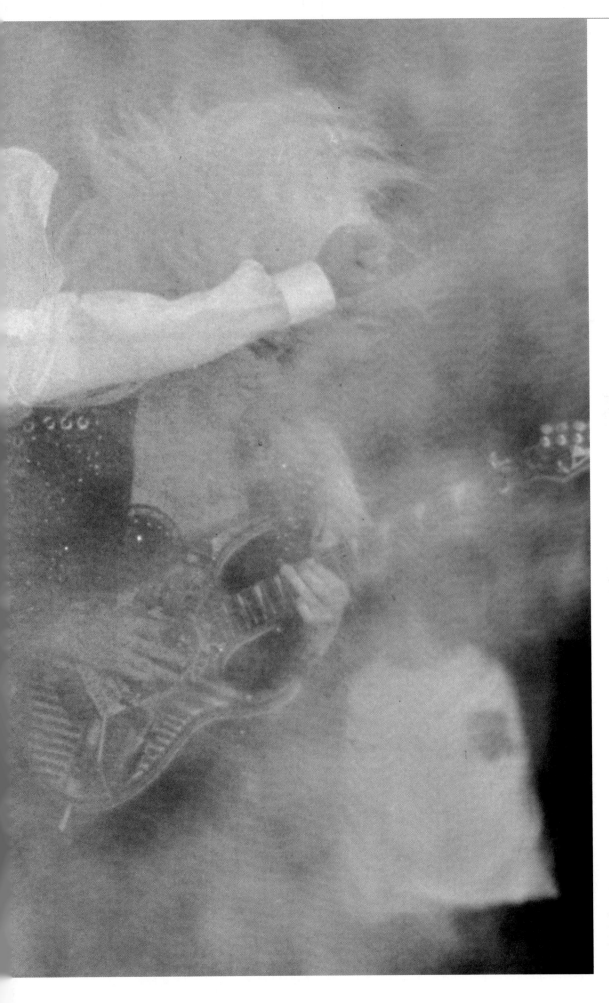

19

Bowling them over:
Michael performing
during the half-time
show at Super Bowl
XXVII in Pasadena,
California in January
1993

Jackson fizz: With his brothers on the set of a Pepsi commercial in 1984

MAKING OF A POP LEGEND...

1. Michael Jackson had 13 number one hits.

2. His album 'Thriller' is the greatest-selling LP of all time. It was the first album ever to outsell Bing Crosby's 'White Christmas' album.

3. Michael Jackson had four number one hits before he was 11 years old.

4. Jackson's chimpanzee chum Bubbles never visited Britain because of strict quarantine laws.

5. Bon Jovi kidnapped Bubbles and took him for a night on the town when Jacko was asleep after a show in Paris. He took the chimp for a boat trip down the Seine.

6. 'Thriller' hit number one in every country in the western hemisphere. It spent a record 33 weeks at the top of the British album charts.

7. Michael Jackson was the first non-Soviet citizen to be featured in a Russian advertising campaign.

8. Jackson was made chief of a village on the African Ivory Coast.

9. In 1992 the South African government banned Jackson's video for 'In The Closet', claiming its sexy content would prove too much for viewers to handle.

10. Filming a Pepsi ad in 1984, Jacko's hair caught fire and he had to be treated for second-degree burns to his skull after a flare accidentally exploded.

11. Jackson tried to buy the skeleton of Elephant Man John Merrick from the London Hospital. He was said to have offered more than $50,000 for Merrick's remains, but it was refused.

12. Michael fought Madonna on M1V's cartoon 'Celebrity Deathmatch' he lost.

13. When he dressed in a wig, false moustache and long overcoat to go shopping in Simi, California, Jackson was arrested in a jewellery store on suspicion of being a shoplifter and ordered to remove his disguise.

14. In 2008, David Gest revealed that when they ate at KFC together, Michael believed that simply peeling off the skin from the fried chicken would make it organic.

15. In 1979, Michael was nominated for a Saturn Award at the Academy of Science Fiction, Fantasy & Horror Films, USA in the category of Best Supporting Actor for his role in the 1978 movie 'The Wiz'.

16. In 1997, Michael joined Luciano Pavarotti and Paul McCartney on a CD tribute to Diana, Princess of Wales.

17. Michael and his brother Tito were co-best men at the Liza Minelli-David Guest wedding.

18. The singer Weird Al has parodied two of Michael's songs: 'Beat It' (which he parodied with 'Eat it') and 'Bad' (which he parodied with 'Fat').

19. Jackson's 'Blood on the Dancefloor' is the biggest-selling re-mix album of all time.

20. Reports of Michael Jackson's death emerged on a showbiz website, sparking a massive surge in online traffic around the globe as millions of people logged on to find out more.

So many people wanted to verify early reports of the singer's death that the computers running Google's news section interpreted the 'Michael Jackson' requests as an automated attack for about half an hour.

Among US users alone, 36 out of the top 100 Google search terms were linked to Jackson's death and his music.

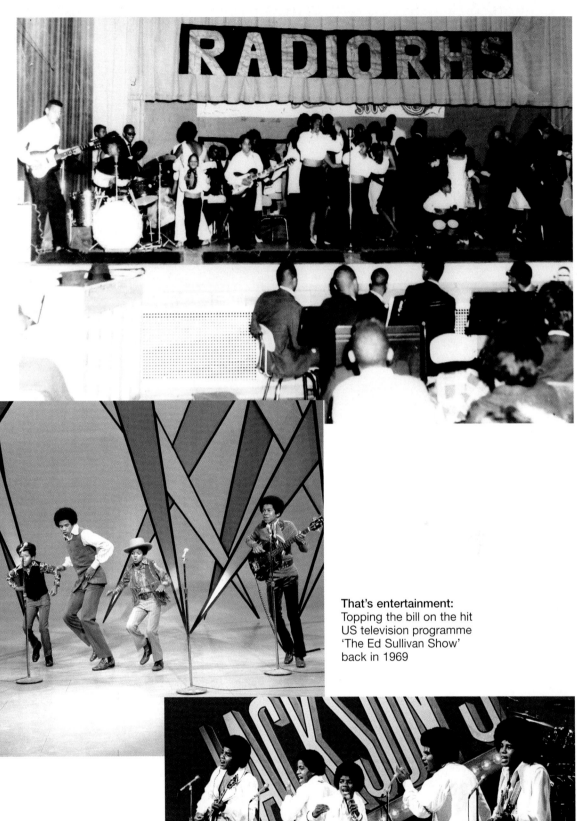

Born performer: On stage with his brothers and, left, preparing to appear on the CBS programme 'The Jackson 5 Show' in October 1972

That's entertainment: Topping the bill on the hit US television programme 'The Ed Sullivan Show' back in 1969

All white on the night: Tito, Marlon, Michael, Jackie and Jermaine perform during the 'Sonny and Cher Comedy Hour' in September 1972

24

Centre stage:
With his brothers in 1970 to
headline another epsode of
'The Ed Sullivan Show'

Mellow yellow:
You couldn't miss Michael during
this Jackson 5 concert in 1975

Home boy:
A 13-year-old Michael in rehearsals with the Jackson 5 at his home in Encino, California, in early 1972

Prince of pop:
A young Michael chats backstage with support group The Commodores

'Fro back:
Wearing a J5 top in 1972

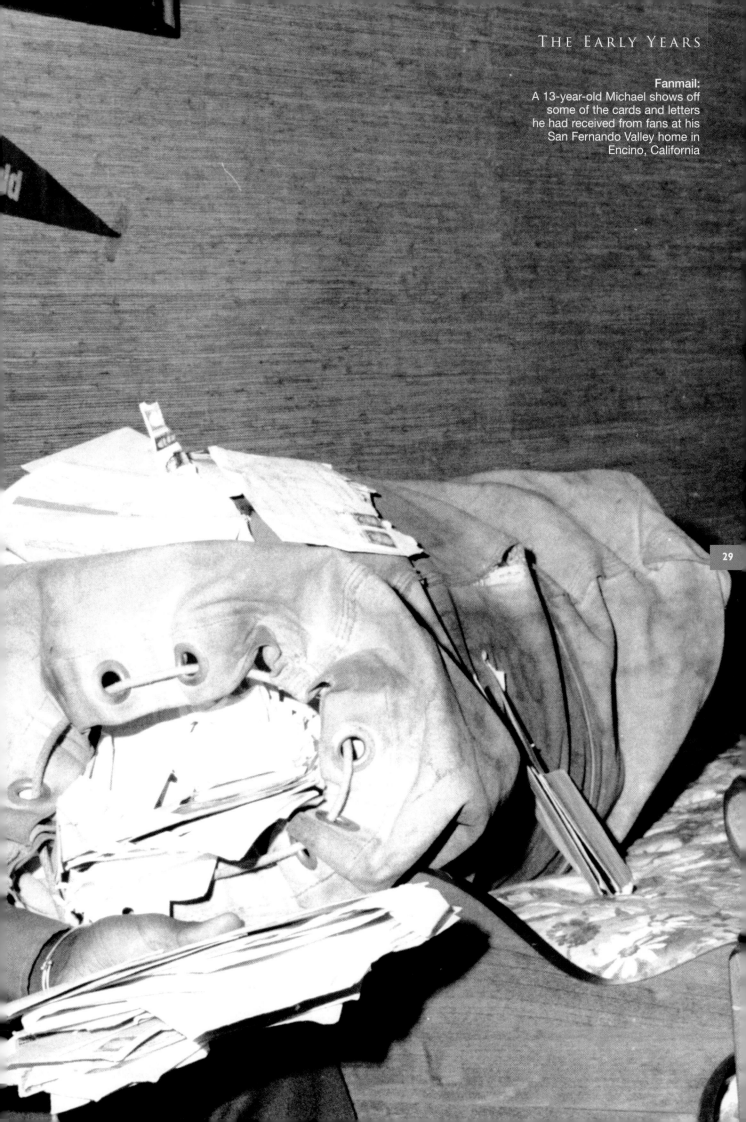

Fanmail:
A 13-year-old Michael shows off some of the cards and letters he had received from fans at his San Fernando Valley home in Encino, California

29

Six appeal: The Jackson 5 with youngest brother Randy in 1972. Randy made several guest appearances with the band, but only officially joined in 1976, when they were renamed The Jacksons

Hitting the heights:
Randy leaps above his
five brothers, from left:
Jackie, Tito, Marlon
Michael and Jermaine

Family affair, below:
La Toya, Rebbie and Janet
Jackson join brothers
Marlon, Randy, Jackie,
Michael and Tito for a
CBS Television Network
variety show in 1976

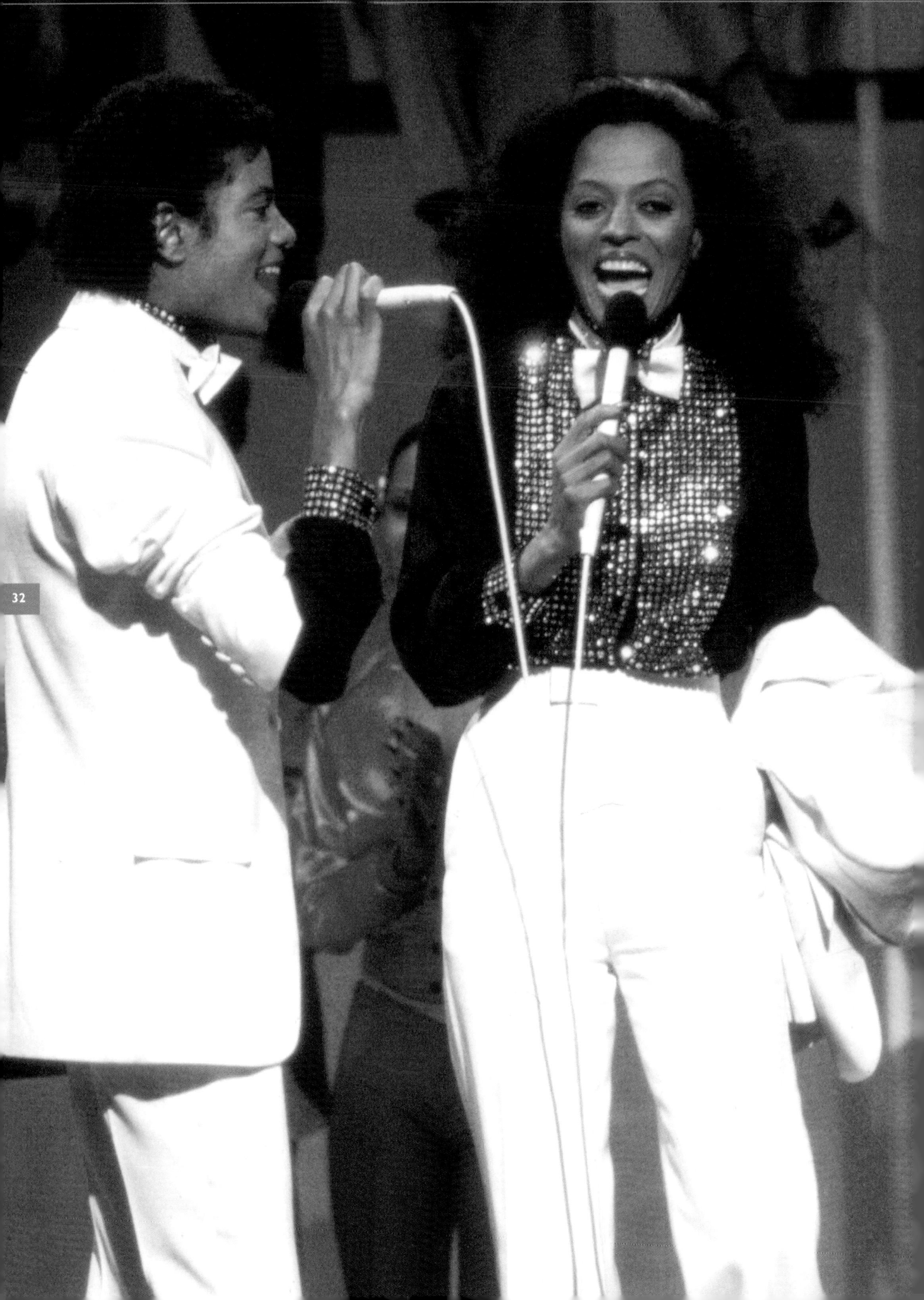

Guest appearance: Michael performing alongside Diana Ross on the CBS television show 'Diana Ross Special' (left) in February 1981, and (above), giving a solo rendition on the same programme

34

Central figure: Performing alongside his brothers in front of 40,000 people at Chicago's Comiskey Park on the Jacksons' Victory Tour in October 1984 – the group's final concert tour. Michael donated all of his reported $5 million proceeds from the 55 shows to charity

Final leg: Dancing on stage in front of 60,000 fans during the Victory Tour in the second of six final Jackson 5 shows at Los Angeles' Dodger Stadium, December 1984

Grammy winner: Showing off his award in the Shrine auditory in Los Angeles, presented for best album of the year for 'Thriller', March 1984

37

38

Main attraction: Michael performing on the Jackson 5's 1984 Victory Tour across the USA and Canada. On the opening leg at Arrowhead Stadium, Kansas City in July (inset), and at Dodger Stadium, Los Angeles in December

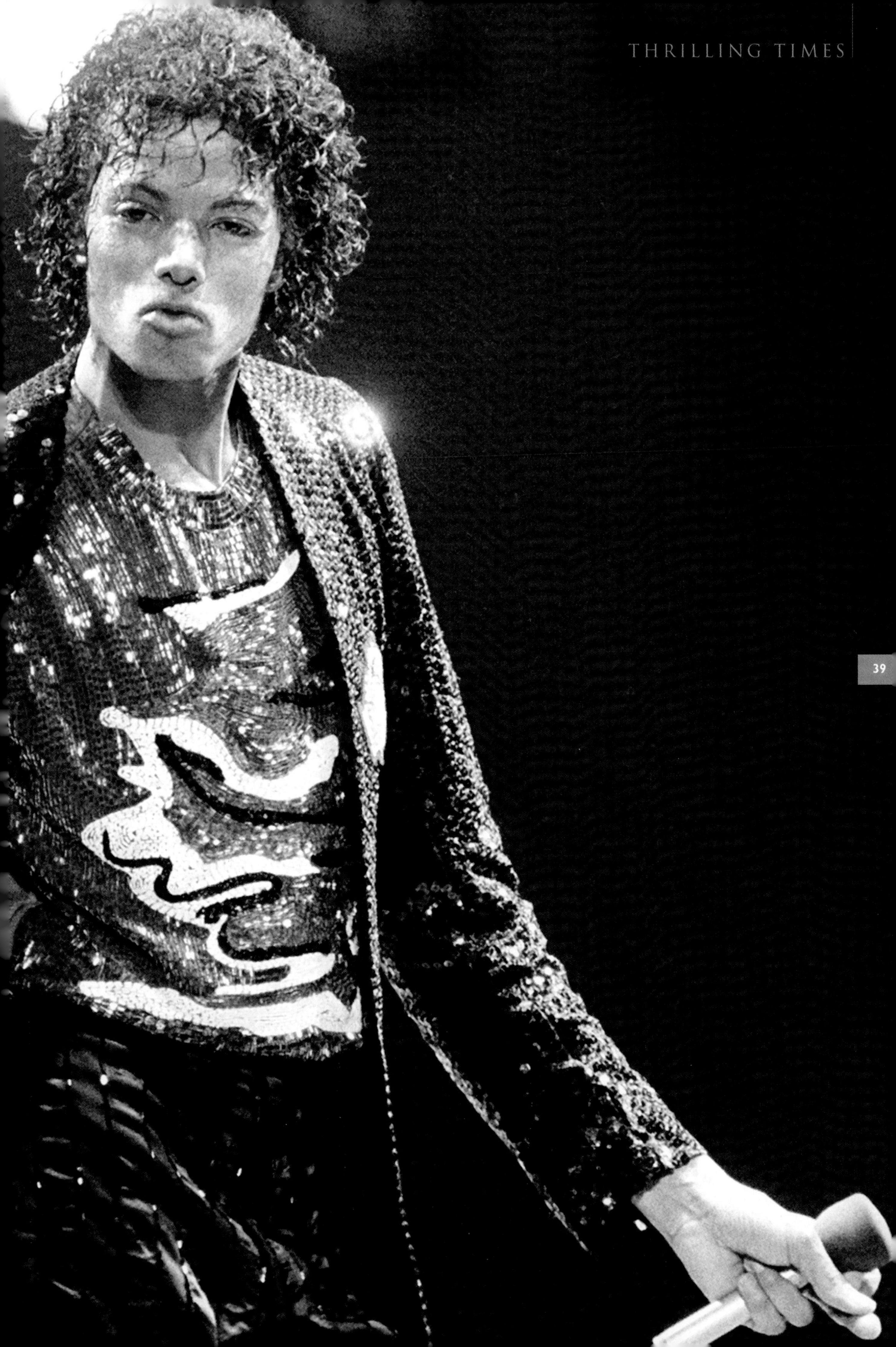

Vintage year: Michael would win eight categories at the 11th Annual American Music Awards of March 1984. He arrived at the Los Angeles ceremony with actress Brooke Shields (left), and was also pictured (below, left to right) with fellow music legends Kenny Rogers, Diana Ross and Barry Manilow. In December of that year on the Victory Tour (opposite page), he performs on the third night of six at Dodger Stadium, Los Angeles with the Jackson 5

40

42

Brothers in arms: Performing on the first night of the Jacksons' Victory Tour at the Arrowhead Stadium, Kansas City in July 1984 (opposite top). Don King looks on as the Jacksons crowd around actor Emmanuel Lewis during a news conference promoting the 1984 Tavern on the Green concert in New York (above). Marlon and Michael performing in Chicago in October 1984 (left). The brothers on the set of a Pepsi commercial (opposite bottom). Left to right: Tito, Jermaine, Jackie, Michael, Randy and Marlon

Jackson salute: Michael hails the audience during the 1984 Victory Tour of USA and Canada

Cop that: The London bobby's helmet proved a hit in 1985. He tried it on when he called on officers at Marylebone Police Station to thank them for protecting him against the enthusiasm of his fans

Sign of the times:
Penning an autograph at his
home in April 1984

Making moves:
Performing on stage at Wembley
during the London leg of the
'Bad' world tour in 1988

48

50

Big in Japan:
Michael dons a red jacket
for a performance of
'Thriller' in Tokyo in 1987

51

You are not alone:
Fans scream and shout at
the Cardiff Arms Park
concert in July 1988 and,
left, stewards take control
amid crowd hysteria at the
Aintree gig in Liverpool

53

Startin' Somethin': At a 1988 concert at Cardiff Arms Park

Showman:
Michael delights fans with
his dance routine during a
performance of 'Dirty
Diana' in July 1988

In the presence of royalty: Michael meeting Princess Diana during his run of Wembley Stadium shows on the Bad World Tour, London, summer 1988

56

Special audience: Princess Diana in conversation with Michael in the summer of 1988. His seven Wembley Stadium shows on the Bad World Tour saw over 500,000 people at the shows

On the prowl:
In 'costume' during the Bad
World Tour at Wembley
Stadium, London, August 1988

59

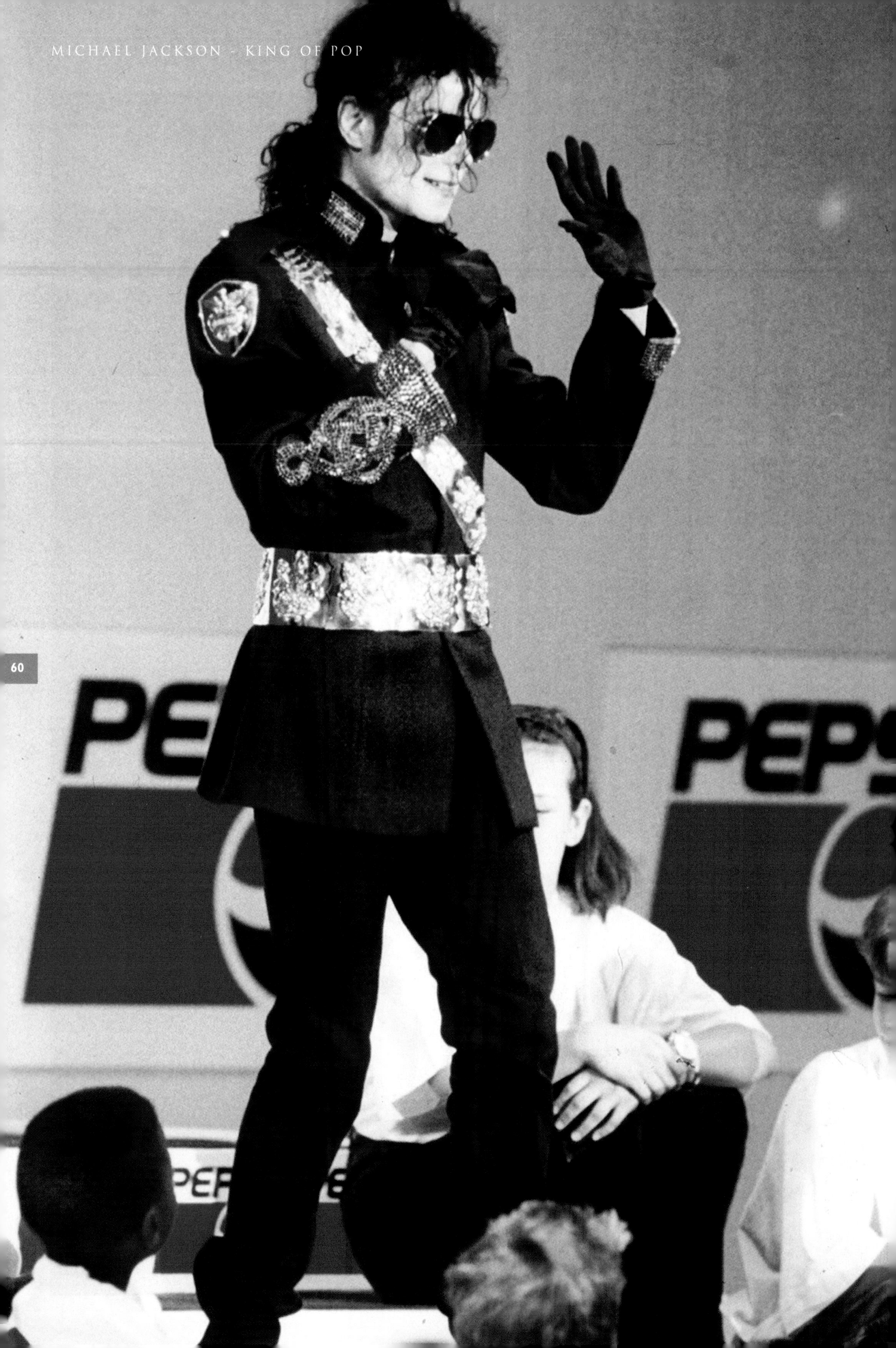

Off the wall:
Being met off the plane by
Mickey and Minnie Mouse
and, below, performing in Italy
in 1992

62

Angel eyes:
On stage in Tokyo
and, opposite, in
front of 70,000
fans in Mexico
City

Glove affair:
Striking a pose during
the 'Dangerous' tour
in Bangkok

66

The girl is mine:
With first wife Lisa
Marie Presley

Mr and Mrs:
Arriving in Hungary
with Lisa Marie in
August 1994

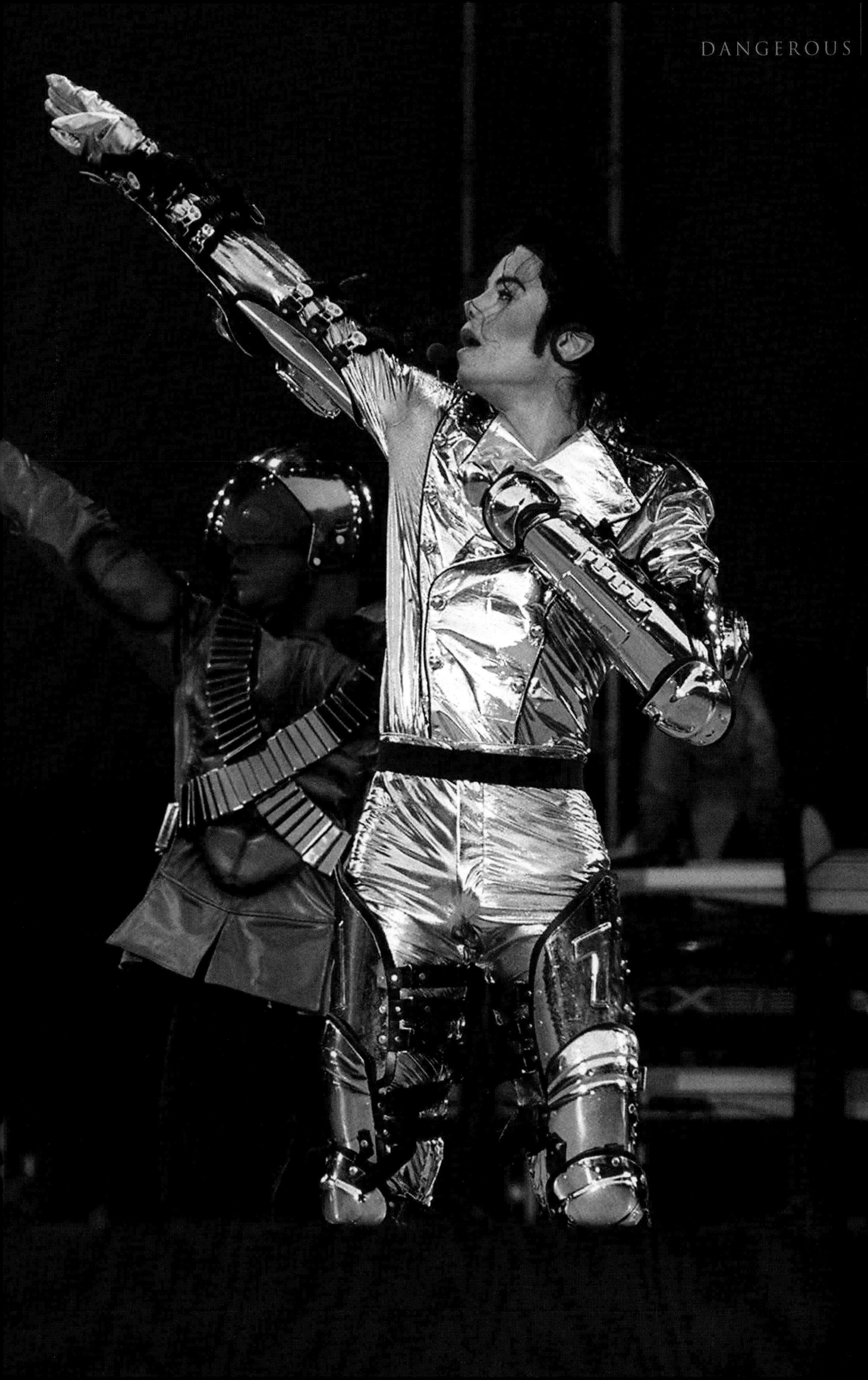

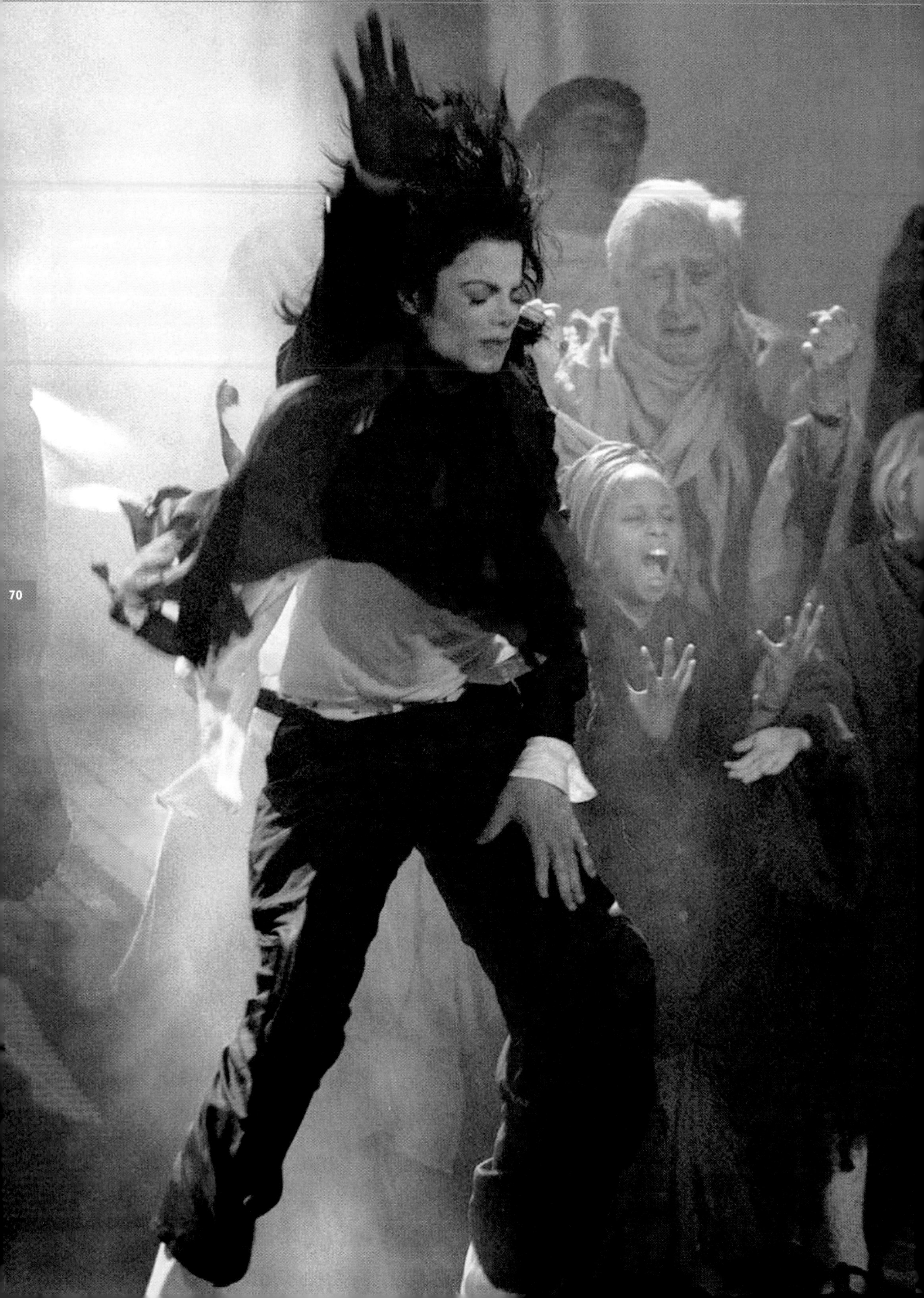

71

At the Brits: Michael performing 'Earth Song' at the Brit Awards in 1996, where he was presented with a special award for being the Artist of a Generation

72

You rock my world:
Performing 'Dangerous' during the recording
of the American Bandstand's 50th anniversary
show in Pasadena in 2002

74

Star quality: Top, with US president Ronald Reagan in 1984. Left, with fellow Grammy winners Dionne Warwick, Stevie Wonder, Quincy Jones and Lionel Richie. Above, Diana Ross introduces the Jackson 5 as they are inducted into the Rock and Roll Hall of Fame. Right, Jackson is mobbed by fans at the World Music Awards at Earls Court in 2006

76

Nearest and dearest:
Opposite, with his pet chimp
Bubbles and his bulldog.
Above, with his great friend
Elizabeth Taylor

I say, say, say:
Joining forces with Paul McCartney
in the recording studio during their
collaborations in the early '80s

78

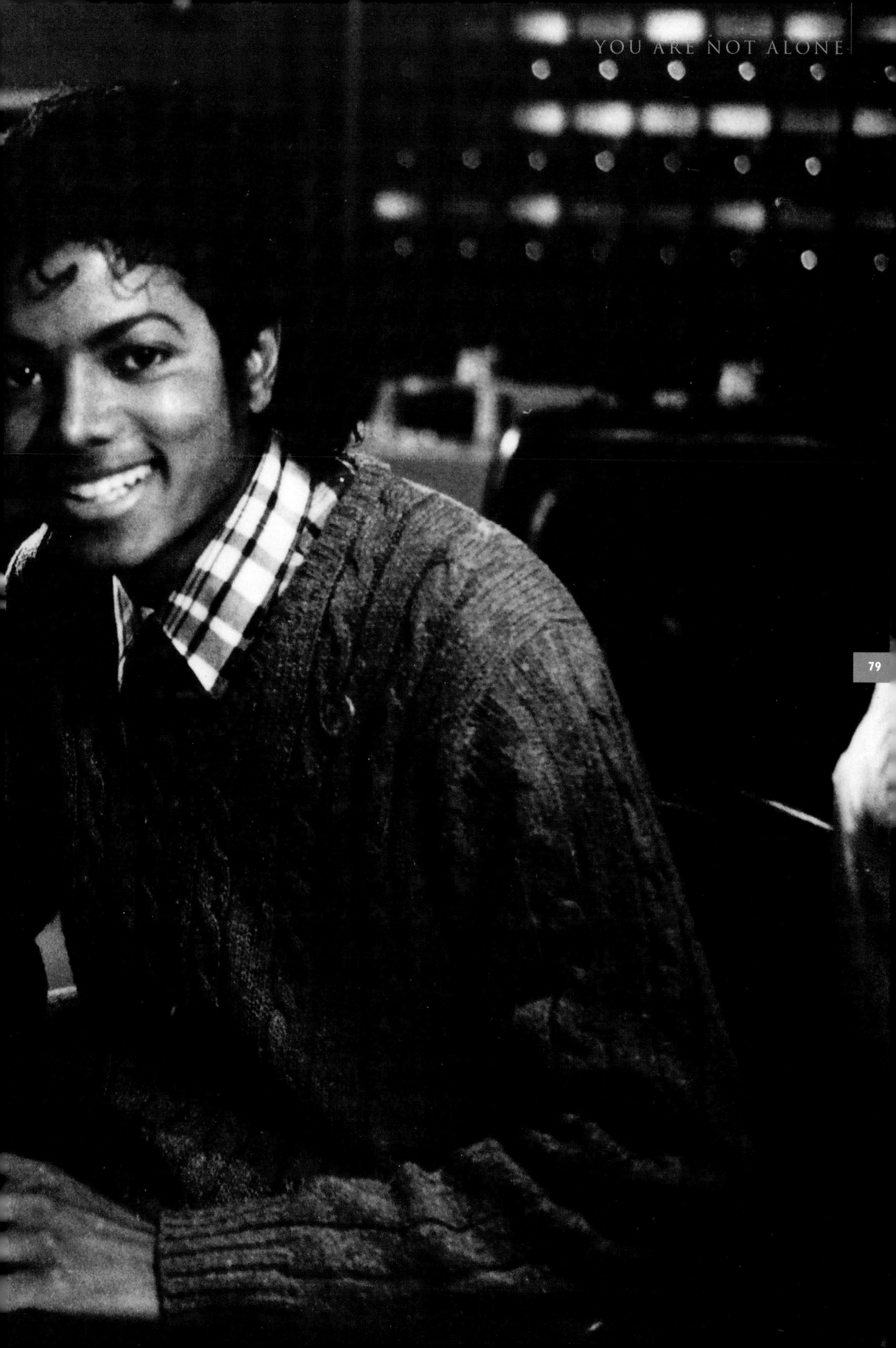

Sister act: Joined on stage by his sisters Rebbie, Janet and La Toya at the 26th Annual Grammy Awards in Los Angeles in 1984

Stage presence:
Twenty years before their hit single 'Scream', Michael joined sister Janet on stage in 1975

DISCOGRAPHY – SOLO ALBUMS

Year	Album	UK Chart position	UK Sales
1972	Got To Be There	37	-
1972	Ben	17	60,000
1979	Off The Wall	5	300,000
1982	Thriller	1	3,300,000
1987	Bad	1	3,900,000
1991	Dangerous	1	1,800,000
1995	HIStory	1	1,500,000
2001	Invincible	1	300,000

DISCOGRAPHY – SOLO SINGLES

Year	Track	UK chart position
1972	Got To Be There	5
1972	Rockin' Robin	3
1972	Ain't No Sunshine	8
1972	Ben	7
1978	Ease On Down The Road*	45
1979	Don't Stop 'Til You Get Enough	3
1979	Off The Wall	7
1980	Rock With You	7
1980	She's Out Of My Life	3
1980	Girlfriend	41
1981	One Day In Your Life	1
1981	We're Almost There	46
1982	The Girl Is Mine**	8
1983	Billie Jean	1
1983	Beat It	3
1983	Wanna Be Startin' Somethin'	8
1983	Happy	52
1983	Thriller	10
1984	P.Y.T.	11
1984	Farewell My Summer Love	7
1984	Girl You're So Together	33
1987	I Just Can't Stop Loving You****	1
1987	Bad	3
1987	The Way You Make Me Feel	3
1988	Man In The Mirror	21
1988	Get It*****	37
1988	Dirty Diana	4
1988	Another Part of Me	15
1988	Smooth Criminal	8
1989	Leave Me Alone	2
1989	Liberian Girl	13
1991	Black Or White	1
1992	Black Or White (re-mix)	14
1992	Remember The Time/Come Together	3
1992	In the Closet	8
1992	Who Is It	10
1992	Jam	13
1992	Heal The World	2
1993	Give In To Me	2
1993	Will You Be There	9
1993	Gone Too Soon	33
1995	Scream******	3
1995	Scream (re-mix)******	43
1995	You Are Not Alone	1
1995	Earth Song	1
1996	They Don't Care About Us	4
1996	Stranger In Moscow	4
1997	Blood On The Dance Floor	1
1997	HIStory/Ghosts	5
2001	You Rock My World	2
2001	Cry	25
2003	One More Chance	5

* with Diana Ross
** with Paul McCartney
*** as USA for Africa
**** with Siedah Garrett
***** with Stevie Wonder
****** with Janet Jackson

MICHAEL JACKSON DISCOGRAPHY – COLLABORATION SINGLES

Year	Track	UK chart position
1978	Ease on Down the Road 1	45
1983	Say Say Say 2	2
1984	Somebody's Watching Me 3	6
1985	We Are The World 4	1
1988	Get It 5	37
1996	Why 6	2
2008	The Girl Is Mine 2008 7	32
2008	Wanna Be Startin' Somethin' 8	69

1 with Diana Ross
2 with Paul McCartney
3 with Rockwell
4 as USA For Africa
5 with Stevie Wonder
6 with 3T
7 with will.i.am
8 with Akon